MIKE YOUNG

SUPERTED

AT THE FUNFAIR

*Illustrations by Rob Lee
and Ian Henderson*

CARNIVAL

In the sick-bay of a very special space station, Spottyman was feeling ill. "Oh dear, SuperTed. I think I've got measles. My spots are disappearing!"

"Yes, Spotty, you do look rather pale today. I'd better take your temperature!"

Suddenly the alarm bell began to sound. "Someone is in trouble, Spotty!" said SuperTed, and he hurried to the video monitor. A woman's face soon appeared on the screen. "SuperTed, I'm very worried, my little boy went to the funfair and hasn't come back. I think he's been kidnapped!"

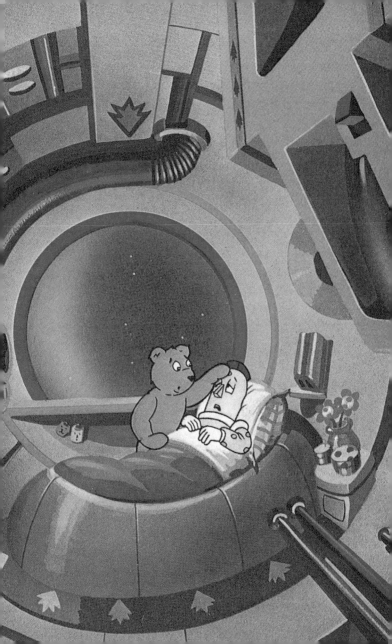

Meanwhile, a small boy called Jonathan was enjoying his last ride of the holiday on the big dipper. "Wheeee!" he screamed, as he rode down a steep slope. Two figures were waiting at the bottom, near a big puddle of water. They were Bulk and Skeleton.

Splash! The car hit the puddle and showered water over the two villains. "Stop it!" shouted Bulk. "Come back here where I can get hold of you!" But by the time he had said this the boy was already halfway up the next slope.

Tex was waiting at the next bend. He hurled his lasso, and it curled neatly round the back of the car. "Yahoo! Got you! Easier than rustling a steer! No-one can handle a lasso quite like Texas Pete!"

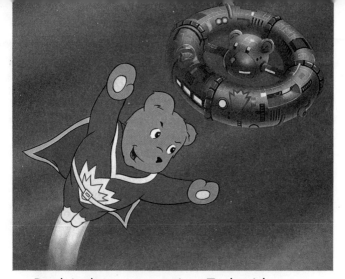

Back in the space station, Ted said
goodbye to the boy's mother and switched
off the monitor. "Pulsating prunes, Spotty! I
think I'd better say my secret magic word!"

In a flash he changed from an ordinary
teddy bear into SuperTed. "Wait for me,
SuperTed," said Spotty, sitting up in bed. "I'll
come with you!"

"Don't be silly, Spotty. You're too ill to get
out of bed. Don't you dare move an inch until
I get home," said SuperTed, and rushed
towards the airlock.

"Do be careful, SuperTed!"

Then the brave teddy bear raced across
the starlit heavens, his rocket boots switched
to full power. His cape flapped in the
emptiness of space, as he turned towards the
planet Earth.

Back at the funfair, Bulk held Jonathan firmly as they made their way between the rides. "I want to go on the waltzer, Tex!" said Bulk, pushing the boy in front of him.

"Are you crazy, Bulk? We're not here to enjoy ourselves."

"What are we here for, Tex?"

"To hide this boy, and then hold him for ransom! Now shut up and stick close to me!"

But they did not stick close to Texas Pete and, as they passed the big wheel, Bulk and Jonathan were scooped into the air in one of the bucket seats. When Skeleton looked up to see what had happened, another bucket hit him.

"Oh, no!" cried Skeleton, "I think I've lost a thigh bone!"

At that very moment, SuperTed flew down
out of the night sky and landed on the big
dipper. "Well this is the funfair, but how am I
going to find the boy? I wish Spotty was here.
It's lonely without him."

Then he caught sight of something
hanging from the lights on the big dipper. It
looked like a rope, but when SuperTed
picked it up he realised at once what it was.
"Texas Pete's lasso! That can mean only one
thing. The boy *has* been kidnapped."

While he stood there wondering what to
do, an empty car hurtled down the track
towards him! With a tremendous jump,
SuperTed hurled himself out of the way, and
swung out over the edge of the big dipper,
clutching onto Texas Pete's lasso.

"Bubbling blancmange! That was close!"

SuperTed swung down from the rope and set off across the funfair.

"Now where would Texas Pete be hiding?" he asked himself. "The shooting gallery? I couldn't see Tex on a roundabout!"

As he was walking along, he tripped over something white and hard that was lying in the dust in front of him. "It's a bone!" he shouted. "It's a thigh bone! Skeleton must have lost it. He'll be hopping around somewhere, hopping mad!"

Then he noticed the ghost train. "I wonder . . . ," he said. That's the perfect hiding place for an evil villain like Texas Pete!"

As SuperTed suspected, Texas Pete and the others were in the ghost train, looking for a suitable place to hide. As they rode through the eerie tunnel, they noticed a fake skeleton, glowing in the dark. Skeleton reached out and grabbed its thigh bone. "Ooo, hello handsome, what's a bone between friends," he said, and tried the bone for size. It was a perfect fit.

Eventually they arrived at a dungeon where a wax model was chained up.

"This looks ideal," drawled Tex. "Bulk! Get rid of that wax model and chain up the boy. Ha ha ha! We'll write a ransom note to the boy's mother. Skeleton you've got fancy handwriting. Write out a ransom note!"

And so Skeleton began to write: "Dear Mum, we've got your boy and we're going to do nasty things to him unless you pay us lots of money. Tex wants a ranch, I need a new pair of slippers and Bulk needs brain surgery."

By now SuperTed had begun to explore the ghost train. He could hear drops of water echoing in the empty tunnel and he was very frightened.

"I do wish that Spotty was here. I don't like being in this ghost train on my own. I wish I'd never come. I wish I was at home, in my tree house, being an ordinary teddy bear."

Then he caught sight of the fake skeleton. "There's only one person who would want a skeleton's thigh bone, and that is Skeleton himself! They must be here!"

The villains were there. As SuperTed came round the next bend, he found Bulk trying to chain Jonathan to the wall.

"Let go of that boy, Bulk!"

"Why should I?" asked Bulk. But almost before he had finished speaking, SuperTed flew towards him and pushed him over.

"Ow! What's this?" cried Bulk. "I think I've been knocked out!"

SuperTed was more worried about Jonathan. "Are you all right? Just be brave for one more minute and I'll be back. Now where's Texas Pete?"

Texas Pete was nowhere to be found. SuperTed looked carefully at the masked dummies that surrounded the dungeon. "Mmm, that nose looks familiar," he said, and he pulled at one of the masks. It came

away in his hand. "That's not him. No, much too handsome."

Then he saw another figure, with evil-looking eyes and a big chin. "Ha Ha!" he shouted. "Now I've got you," and he caught hold of Texas Pete's nose.

"Ow, not my nose, let me go."

"Come along Tex. You always did have a nose for trouble!"

As they all rode back towards the entrance to the ghost train, SuperTed noticed that there were now two skeletons in the tunnel. One of them was wearing slippers.

"Come along, Skeleton," said SuperTed, "I know it's you."

"Oh, can't I stay with my friend?"

"No, you're coming with us," ordered SuperTed, and Skeleton sheepishly climbed into the car.

Later, back in the space station, SuperTed told Spotty what had happened.

"Well, Spotty, you're looking much better. Your spots are coming back. Here, I've brought you this photograph from the fair."

"Thanks, SuperTed, I would have given all the moons of Spot to have gone to the funfair!"

When Spotty looked at the photograph he laughed and laughed. There were the three villains looking sillier than ever!

MIKE YOUNG

SUPERTED

AND THE ELEPHANTS' GRAVEYARD

*Illustrations by Chris Fenna
and Ian Henderson*

Across the grasslands of East Africa you can
see the distant mountains and the snow on
the tops sparkles in the sunlight. An elephant
is making its way slowly over the plains
towards the place were all elephants who
have lived a full and happy life go to die: the
Elephants' Graveyard. But the elephant's
journey is being watched by evil eyes. Texas
Pete, Bulk and Skeleton look on.

The long grass has given Bulk hay fever
and he begins to sneeze, "A.a.a.a. . ."

Tex is irritated. "Shut up, Bulk. Keep your
eyes on that elephant, it'll lead us to a fortune
in ivory."

Bulk has never heard of ivory. "Ivory?
What's ivory, Tex?"

Skeleton knows the answer. "Bones.
Great, big, whopping elephant bones . . .
lovely."

Meanwhile, beneath a treehouse deep in the woods, Spottyman a young space traveller from another galaxy, is sleeping away a warm summer's afternoon, when an elephant's trunk appears from around the tree and nudges him awake.

"Great moons of Spot! It's a nightmare! A horrible spotless nightmare."

Ted is a friend of all the animals and understands them. "No, Spotty. It's only an elephant. He has come all the way from Africa. Someone is trying to steal all the ivory from the Elephants' Graveyard."

Spotty is amazed. "Why would someone want to steal ivory?"

Ted explains. "People use it to make knife handles, piano keys, that kind of thing. I'll say my magic word and we'll use your rocket ship. Let's go."

Back in Africa, the three villains are making their way through the grass.

Bulk's nose is twitching. "A.a.a.a."

Tex hisses a command, "Quiet Bulk."

"I can't help it Tex, it's hay fever, a.a.a.a."

At that moment a leopard is also stalking through the grass.

Skeleton is enjoying himself, "Lot's of lovely wild plants and animals," he says.

The leopard is about to pounce when Bulk's nose twitches. He sneezes. The leopard scuttles away frightened.

The baddies follow the old elephant who arrives in front of a cliff. Cascading down the centre is a tremendous waterfall. The elephant slowly plods through the waterfall into his secret resting place. Texas Pete, Bulk and Skeleton follow him through.

Tex gloats, "Boys, we've struck it rich!"

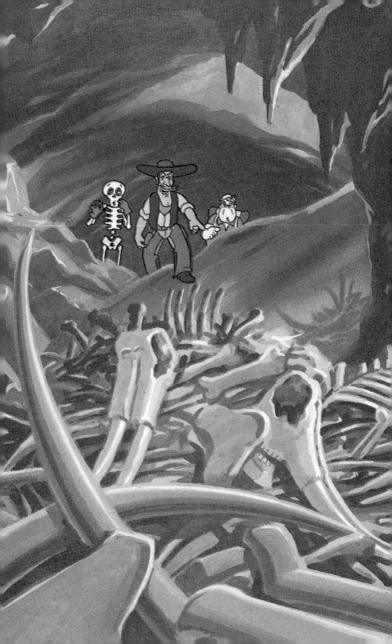

The Spotty rocketship has landed in the grasslands. SuperTed, Spotty and the elephant have climbed out. SuperTed looks about him. "Well, where do we go now? There's nothing here but a sheer rock face. Look out, Spotty a leopard."

Spotty is delighted, "It's a cat, a lovely spotty pussy cat. I haven't seen one of those since I left the planet Spot. Come here, Spottles."

Even SuperTed is a little worried. "Spottles? Careful Spotty it could be dangerous!"

Spottyman plays with the leopard. "There's a lovely pussy cat. All right off you go, Spottles."

The leopard heads towards the waterfall and walks straight through.

"Did you see that, Spotty? I think it's the entrance to the Elephants' Graveyard. Come on."

They follow the leopard to the waterfall.
They pass through it and find themselves in a
gigantic cavern, filled with the most
beautiful, strange rock shapes. SuperTed,
Spotty and the elephant make their way
forward.

Spottyman whispers, "I don't like it,
SuperTed. It's a bit eerie, maybe we should
go back."

SuperTed feels frightened too, but bravely
says, "No, Spotty, we must keep going . . .
Look!"

They turn a corner and find themselves in
an even larger cave with a flat floor. It is lit by
a narrow slit of light, coming from a crack in
the ceiling. There are stacks of the bones and
tusks of hundreds of elephants.

Just then SuperTed spots Bulk. "He's getting away. Quick! Get Bulk, Spotty."

Bulk scrambles up a pile of bones which collapse and cover him and SuperTed.

Spotty is concerned, "SuperTed, where are you?"

"I'm under here, don't worry, no bones broken. Where's Bulk?"

"A.a.a.tchoo." A giant sneeze shifts the bones to reveal Bulk. "I'm not here, really. This isn't really me. I'm invisible. Get me?"

"Yes get him Spotty I'll go after Tex and Skeleton."

Skeleton has craftily hidden himself amongst the bones. He sings to himself, "Dem bones, dem bones, dem dry bones."

Through in the next cavern the old elephant is tied up with a lasso. Tex has disappeared through the crack in the ceiling. He struggles onto the cliff outside carrying a huge ivory tusk. "Heh, heh, heh. Guess I was a little too quick for that puny teddy bear."

From behind him comes a voice he knows only too well. "That's what *you* think, Texas Pete."

Tex splutters a threat. "Don't come too close, SuperTed. This tusk could cut you to the bone. Get the point?"

SuperTed dodges the sharp point, catches the tusk, and pulls Texas Pete over the cliff and the waterfall. Then he lands in the pool at the bottom and seconds later, SuperTed shouts out, "There's nothing like a cold shower to cool you down."

The elephant dips his trunk into the water and pulls Tex out.

SuperTed zooms off and flies over the grassland, looking for Skeleton. In a clearing, he finds him frightened and on his knees begging for mercy. In front of him the leopard is licking his lips. SuperTed lands and takes over, he'll take care of Skeleton.

Much later, SuperTed is happy to have solved another mystery. "Well Spotty. I don't think anyone will disturb the elephants again."

Spotty is about to speak when . . . "A.a.a.tchoo!" he sneezes. It seems that Spottymen get hay fever too.

Carnival
An imprint of the Children's Division
of the Collins Publishing Group
8 Grafton Street, London W1X 3LA

Published by Carnival 1988

Based on scripts written by
ROBIN LYONS

Cartoon films as seen on BBC and
S4C Television, produced by Siriol
Animation for S4C, the Welsh Fourth Channel

Printed & bound in Great Britain by
PURNELL BOOK PRODUCTION LIMITED
A MEMBER OF BPCC plc